THE DREAMCATCHER

Keep your happy dreams forever!

Written by

Jasmine Brook and Lianne McCabe

Illustrated by Helen Cann

SMITHMARK

What are dreams?

When we dream, we unlock our imaginations and the "unconscious" part of our brain, the part that works when we are asleep. Some people believe that dreaming may just be our mind's way of sorting out the thoughts that we have during the day. Others believe that our dreams can tell us all kinds of things about ourselves, our past and even our future.

To the Native Americans, dreaming was a very important part of life. They believed that a "Sacred Power" would speak to them in dreams. This power or spirit would often appear as an animal, maybe an eagle, buffalo or a bear. Sometimes, dreams could be very mysterious and only the tribe's medicine man, called a "shaman," would be able to tell what they meant.

The Native Americans believed that they could learn much from their dreams. If our dreams can teach us more about ourselves, just imagine what we could discover if we learn to understand them!

What is a Dreamcatcher?

Dreamcatchers come in
many shapes and sizes.
They are very bright and
colorful and can be hung
anywhere in the house
for good luck.

The Native Americans invented the dreamcatcher many
years ago. They believe that good dreams pass through the
dreamcatcher, while bad dreams get caught in the web
and disappear.

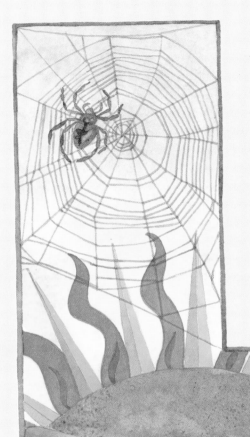

In the center of the dreamcatcher's web you will sometimes find a colored bead. This bead is said to represent a spider. Some Native Americans believe the spider kills bad dreams. Others believe bad dreams are caught in the web and disappear when the sun comes up. The Native Americans call the spider "Iktome," or "The Keeper of Dreams."

You can add a spider to your own dreamcatcher. All you need to do is place a colored bead at the center of the web and you'll have your very own Keeper of Dreams!

The Dreamcatcher

Dreamcatchers are given to Native American newborn babies. As the child grows, the dreamcatcher becomes more important in their life. On a larger dreamcatcher, an eagle feather might be added, to show an important battle won. They might also hang a tooth from an animal killed while hunting. The dreamcatcher becomes a display of the child's good memories as they grow.

Today, larger dreamcatchers are decorated with things that are easier to come by! Anything that has special meaning can be added. Sea shells, dried flowers, favorite photographs, anything at all!

The Native Americans blessed their dreamcatcher to give it extra power. To bless your dreamcatcher, all you have to do is to think of something that is special to you. It could be your Mom and Dad, or even your pet. All you need to say is, "I bless this dreamcatcher with . . ."

Now that you have your very own dreamcatcher, you can add your own special blessing to it. May it bring you lots of happy dreams!

Journey of Dreams

"Dana Daydreamer! Dana Daydreamer!" came the taunts,
followed by laughter as the school gates opened. Dana walked
on alone to her favorite place, the dream place. Here she
could sit, gaze across the valley, and daydream of
all the wonderful things that, one day, she would do.

"Hello, daydreamer!" A shadow crossed Dana and she looked up to see Sam smiling down at her. Sam was River Creek's living legend, the last of the Native Americans in these parts, and her only real friend. "What are you dreaming about today?" he asked as he sat down.

"I'm not dreaming," Dana replied. "I'm wishing. I'm wishing that I was anyone but me."

"Hold on to your dreams instead," smiled Sam. "Dreams are so much better than wishes. Your dreams make you special, Dana."

He reached into his pocket and held out his hand. In his palm was a strange-looking circle of string, woven with beads and fabric. "This is for you, Dana Daydreamer," he said. "It will help you hold on to your dreams."

Dana took the gift in her hand, and turned it over. "What is it?" she asked.

"It's a dreamcatcher," Sam replied. "It lets your good dreams pass through and catches the bad."

Later, Dana stared up at the dreamcatcher she'd hung over her bed. As it twirled above, her eyes slowly shut and she began to dream. . . .

She was racing across the plains. She rode a white horse and beside her was a boy, his hair as jet black as his horse. "Faster!" he called back at her. He laughed and raced ahead, across the dusty earth, past the buffalo and wild horses. Dana whipped her reins and whispered to her horse, "Faster!"

Together, they flew across the ground, as free as clouds. As they neared a village, the boy signaled to her to stop. "We're here!" he called to Dana, and sprung from his horse.

Leaving her horse too, Dana followed the boy to the village center. Silence hung in the air and the boy's words echoed as he spoke, "The shaman is here." Into the heart of the village crowd strode an old, gray-haired man. He carried a staff and his face was as lined and cracked as the sun-scorched earth itself.

He paused in front of the glowing fire and looked straight ahead. "Closer," he beckoned to Dana. Dana moved slowly forward, looking to her friend for guidance, and stopped in front of the shaman. He looked down, touched her lightly on the shoulder, and spoke.

"Dream Child," he said, "yours is the gift of dreams. The gift of thought and the gift of sight without seeing. Hold on to your dreams, they will take you wherever you wish to go."

From around his neck, the shaman took a string of beads, some turquoise and some red. All glistened in the moonlight. He placed the necklace around Dana's neck. "Hold on to your dreams," he repeated. Then he smiled, "They will show you all you can be."

The morning light shone through the curtains and crossed Dana's sleeping face. Slowly, her eyes opened and, as something glinted, she looked up. At the very heart of the dreamcatcher hung a necklace. A necklace made of beads, some turquoise and some red. All glistened in the sunlight.

"My dream!" Dana breathed. "The necklace from my dream!"

Dana clutched the dreamcatcher in amazement. She needed to think and the dream place was the only place to go. As Dana sat and wondered at her dream, a shadow crossed her and she looked up to see Sam.

"Sam," she breathed as she held out her dreamcatcher. He smiled as he saw the necklace at its center.

"Dreams are more powerful than you know, Dana," he said. "They hold all our wishes, hopes and thoughts. Sometimes I think they are more real than ourselves."

He sat down beside her and took the dreamcatcher in his hands. It was then that Dana recognized the necklace around Sam's neck. It was just the same as the boy's in her dream!

Sam smiled at her puzzled face and handed back the dreamcatcher. "Hold on to your dreams, Dana," he whispered. "They'll take you wherever you wish to go."

The Keeper of Dreams

Lucy was reading aloud from one of her favorite wildlife books. "Arachnaphobia is a fear of spiders, but in reality, most spiders serve us well and do us little harm."

Jason wasn't convinced. For as long as he could remember, he had been frightened of spiders. Recently, these fears had taken shape as bad dreams, too. "I don't like living here," he said. "There weren't as many spiders in the city."

They had left the city to start a new life on Iktome Ranch, their mother's childhood home. Lucy and her mother hadn't liked the harshness of city life and had longed to return to Iktome's wild landscape. They hoped that Jason's bad dreams would disappear in this peaceful place and that he would come to love Iktome, too.

Lucy shut her book. "Let's explore!" she said, and ran outside. Jason followed sullenly behind. In the yard, their grandfather waved to them. "When your mother was a little girl, she would explore the caves on a fine day like this," he said.

"Mom says the caves are full of spiders," Jason replied.

"Well, the cave spiders won't hurt you," Grandfather chuckled. "You'll find Iktome's land has many mysteries, and if you treat it well, it'll do the same for you."

Jason followed Lucy across the fields, towards Iktome Cave. "Mom says that the Native Americans came to the cave to dream "Power Dreams," dreams of great prophecy and meaning," Lucy called. "The cave was a sacred place, because of Iktome."

Jason looked puzzled. "The Keeper of Dreams!" Lucy explained. "Iktome is the spider at the center of all dream-catchers. It lets your good dreams pass through, but it catches the bad and destroys them."

"Spiders don't protect you!" said Jason.

"Well, Mom says it's true," Lucy replied. "I don't believe in all that, but you're such a dreamer, you'll probably have a "Power Dream" too!"

Suddenly, Lucy stopped chattering and looked up. There before them was an enormous cave. "Iktome Cave!" she shouted and raced inside. Jason ventured into the cave's entrance. "I'll wait here," he called as Lucy ran ahead.

Across the cave walls were endless pictures, carved many years before by the Native Americans. Even now the colors were still dazzling. And at the center of the paintings was the image of a Native American, within a circle of spiders.

The quiet was calming, and Jason didn't feel as frightened as he had. He sat down, rested his head against a rock and, just for a moment, closed his eyes.

As Jason's eyes opened, the Native American seemed to speak: "Iktome, guard our good dreams and destroy the bad!" Jason closed his eyes again, and it seemed to him that he started to dream.

Around the circle of spiders many pictures moved. Some showed joyful events and some showed sad. But only the happy scenes passed inside the circle. The spiders seemed to be protecting him from his bad dreams!

As he sat and watched the circle of spiders, Jason felt no fear at all and for the first time, his phobia disappeared.

"Jason!" Lucy's voice broke the silence and the wall painting became still again. "I've been all the way through the cave while you've been sitting here!"

"I saw something," Jason said. "Iktome, The Keeper of Dreams!"

The Keeper of Dreams

"You know I don't believe in all that!" scoffed Lucy. "Come on, it's getting dark." They walked slowly through the fields, back to the ranch where Mom was waiting. "Jason had a "Power Dream!" Lucy laughed as she raced past into the ranch house.

"Did you see the spiders, Jason?" his mother asked. Jason rested with her against the ranch gate. At its center, a spider's web sparkled in the evening sunlight.

"I'm not sure," he replied, "but I don't think I'll be having any more bad dreams!"

"Iktome will keep all our dreams sweet," his mother smiled.

And together they watched the sun set over Iktome Mountain.

Dream of the Great Bear

I slept beneath the stars' beacon light
I saw Great Bear run through the night
He growled at the moon
He clawed at the dark
He chased through the comet's flaming spark

I followed him to the comet's rainbow
I saw Great Bear dance in its colored glow
We swooped through red
We danced through white
We raced together through the night

I soared up to the glowing moon's shape
I saw Great Bear leaping in its silver lake
We floated in its rise
We rested in its fall
We played as first dawnlight sparkled on all

I laughed as the shooting star spun away
I saw Great Bear follow its trail, to day
He leapt over clouds
He brushed past the sun
He called me to see that the morning had come

I slept beneath the stars' beacon light
I saw Great Bear run through the night
We danced with the comet
We rested on the moon
When night comes again, I'll see Great Bear soon.

Your Dream Diary

So important were dreams to the Native Americans that they would journey to sacred places, often mountain tops, to try to conjure up the "spirits" through dream.

Some dreams were thought to be of little importance and were quickly forgotten. Other dreams were thought to be "Power Dreams," dreams in which the Sacred Power spoke. These dreams were analyzed in great detail by the shaman and the dreamer, until they felt that they knew their true meaning.

Like the Native Americans, we too can try to discover what our dreams mean by keeping a dream diary. Even though we dream every night, we can't always remember our dreams, or we forget them very quickly after waking! A dream diary can help us to remember.

How to Keep Your Dream Diary

To keep a dream diary, all you need is a notebook or a diary. As soon as you wake each morning, write down what you can remember about your dream. There are certain things to look out for:

The Date
Always write down the date of your dream. This will help you to look back through your diary and see if you have dreamed a dream before, or to see if your dream came true!

Feelings
Write down how you felt in your dream. Was your dream exciting, frightening or happy?

Your Dream Theme
Every dream has a "theme."
You might be on a journey,
or you might be searching for something. Write down what you think the theme of your dream was.

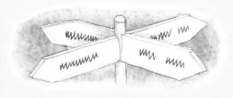

People and Signs
Did any people, objects or signs appear in your dream? Signs are often "signposts" that can guide us through life.

Journeys
Write down if you traveled anywhere in your dream.

The journeys that we take in our dreams often show us the "path" that we take through life.

Now that you know what to look for in your dreams, you can begin to figure out what they mean! Remember, you know better than anyone your dreams' true meanings.

KEEP HOLD OF YOUR HAPPY DREAMS FOREVER!